BiOBLiTZ!

For my husband, Jim, with whom every walk
in the park becomes a joyful adventure!
—S. E. R.

For Debbie and Emma
—S. F. C.

Published by
PEACHTREE PUBLISHING COMPANY INC.
1700 Chattahoochee Avenue
Atlanta, Georgia 30318-2112
PeachtreeBooks.com

Text © 2022 by Susan Edwards Richmond
Illustrations © 2022 by Stephanie Fizer Coleman

Edited by Vicky Holifield
Design and composition by Adela Pons

The illustrations were rendered digitally.

Printed and bound in June 2022 at C&C Offset, Shenzhen, China.
10 9 8 7 6 5 4 3 2 1
First Edition
ISBN: 978-1-68263-311-3

Cataloging-in-Publication Data is available from the Library of
Congress.

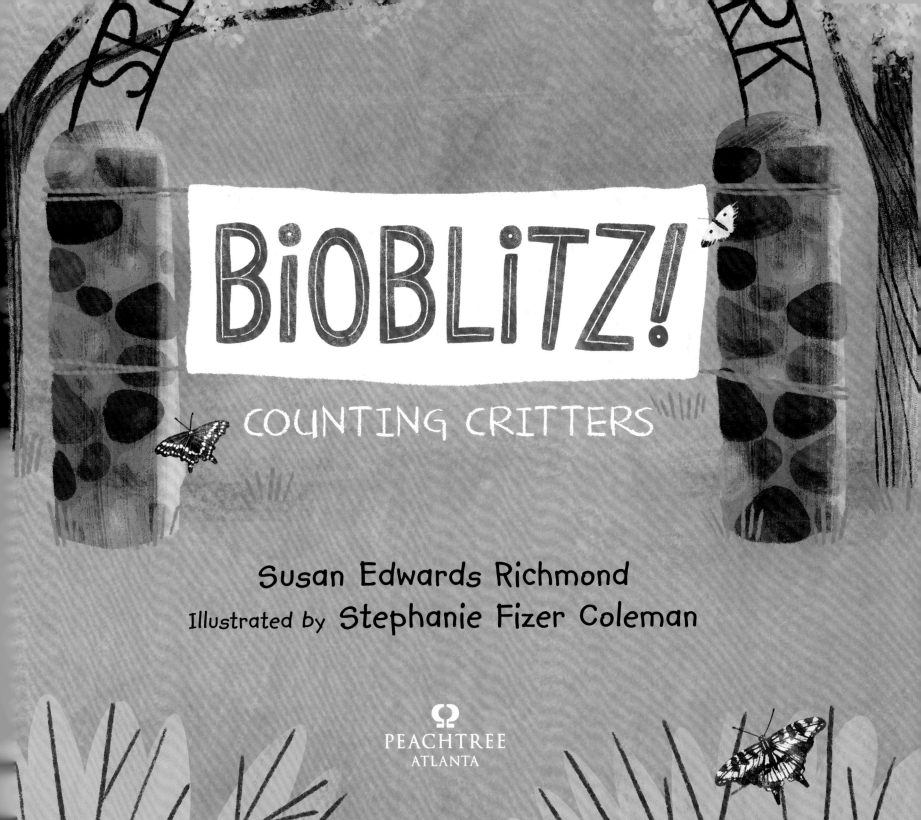

BiOBLiTZ!

COUNTING CRITTERS

Susan Edwards Richmond

Illustrated by Stephanie Fizer Coleman

PEACHTREE
ATLANTA

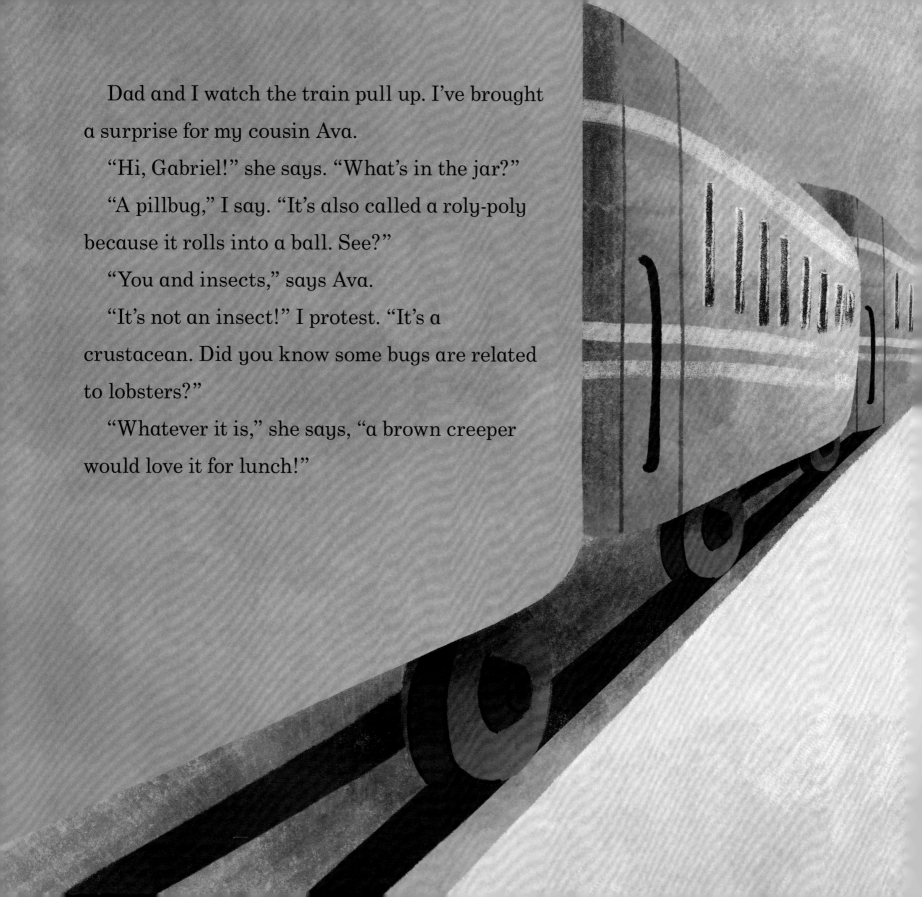

Dad and I watch the train pull up. I've brought a surprise for my cousin Ava.

"Hi, Gabriel!" she says. "What's in the jar?"

"A pillbug," I say. "It's also called a roly-poly because it rolls into a ball. See?"

"You and insects," says Ava.

"It's not an insect!" I protest. "It's a crustacean. Did you know some bugs are related to lobsters?"

"Whatever it is," she says, "a brown creeper would love it for lunch!"

"Before you start a birds versus bugs battle," says Dad, "I have a surprise, too. Spring Meadow Park is holding its first Bioblitz tomorrow. I've signed us up."

"What's a Bioblitz?" I ask.

"It's a count of all the different living things, or *species*, in an area," says Dad. "Some Bioblitzes look for plants *and* animals. Ours is just critters."

"Birds, too?" asks Ava.

"Birds, too," says Dad. "That's why we need you!"

When we arrive the next morning, Ranger Kai says, "Welcome, community scientists!"

"That's us," I whisper to Ava.

"Just a few rules," says Ranger Kai. "We'll split into two teams. I'll lead the Green Team. Ranger Leo will lead the Blue."

"Hey, that's your dad!" says Ava.

"Each team will keep a list of the animal species they see or hear," Ranger Kai tells us. "And we'll take a picture of each new species we find. If we can't take a picture, at least two people need to see or hear it."

"Just like a bird count!" says Ava.

"Right," says Dad. "Every species counts."

Ranger Kai nods. "At the end of the day, we'll combine both lists."

"Look!" I shout as an orange-patterned butterfly wings past. "A **great spangled fritillary**!"

Ranger Kai gives me a wink. "You're with me, Gabriel."

Ava, who's on Dad's team, is already pointing out a bird.

"Bet our team finds more!" I call to her.

"You're on!"

"Gabriel, why don't you keep the species list for our team?" asks Ranger Kai.

I'm excited to have an important job on my first Bioblitz.

"I'll take the pictures," she continues. "Mrs. Tatke, will you help out with your field guide?"

"Love to," Mrs. Tatke replies.

Our first stop is the edge of the ball field. I see an insect on a blade of grass.

"**Meadow spittlebug**!" I call to Ranger Kai. "Did you know spittlebugs cover their eggs in bubbly spit?"

"Nice!" says Ranger Kai. *Click.* She snaps a photo with her phone.

Other team members find a **cricket**, a **sparrow**, a **katydid**, and other animals. I write them all down and draw the robin for Ava.

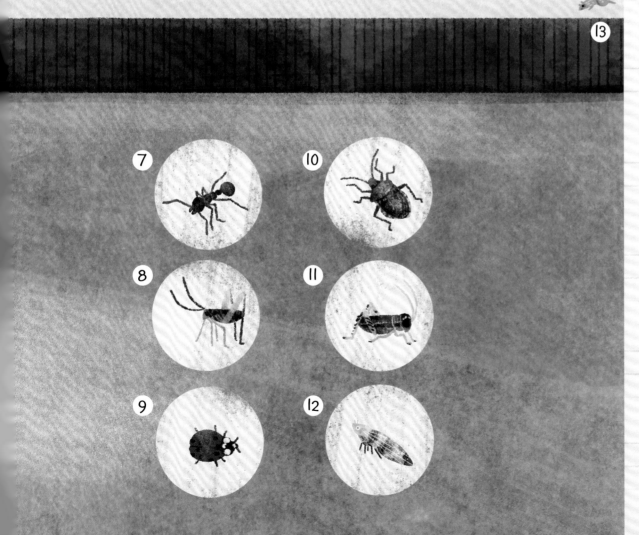

AMERICAN ROBIN

"Let's look in the butterfly garden," says
Ranger Kai.

"**Eastern tiger swallowtail!**" shouts one of
our team members.

"**Monarch!**" says another.

Click. Click.

I watch a **bumblebee** shoulder aside **honeybees** on a Joe-Pye weed. Then something else swoops in. "Is that a hummingbird?" I ask.

But up close I can see that it's not a bird at all. "**Hummingbird moth**!" I shout. "Hey, Ranger Kai. Did you know some bugs look like birds?"

"Good ID!" she says. "See the fringy antennae, everyone?"

"There's a real bird," I say, pointing to a **goldfinch**. Ava would be proud of me!

HUMMINGBIRD MOTH

Sunlight sparkles on the lily pond. A fin splashes near shore, causing two **mallards** to fly.

"That's a **brown bullhead**," says Ranger Kai.

"I hear a banjo twang!" says Mrs. Tatke.

"**Green frog**," says Ranger Kai. "Thank you for reminding us to listen as well as look."

Ranger Kai scoops up water in a tub. A **water strider**, a **water boatman**, and a **whirligig beetle** dart and swirl.

"What's that?" I point to what looks like a bundle of twigs shuffling across the bottom.

"A **caddisfly** larva," says Ranger Kai. "It covers itself with pond debris for protection."

29

31

30

27

28

32

"Great camouflage," I say. "Did you know that an insect called the lacewing uses aphids' dead bodies to hide itself?"

"Yuck," says Mrs. Tatke.

BROWN BULLHEAD

"Let's head for the picnic grove," says Ranger Kai. "The Blue Team will join us soon. We'll look and listen while we eat."

A **red squirrel** searches for crumbs under our table. A tiny bird looks for beetles on a tree trunk. Ranger Kai tells us it is a **red-breasted nuthatch**.

Then we hear a funny *chirrrr.* "What's that?" someone asks. "A giant insect?"

"Not an insect," says Ranger Kai. "But it would sure like to eat some! That's a **red-bellied woodpecker**. "

As I pick up my sandwich, a **jumping spider** hops over. "Did you know a jumping spider has four pairs of eyes?" I ask Ranger Kai.

"I guess that's how it knew you had the best lunch," she says.

38

39

40

41

42

A **deer fly** lands on my arm. "Can I brush it off?" I ask.

"As long as we identify it first," says Ranger Kai.

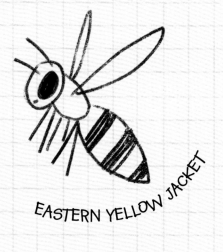

EASTERN YELLOW JACKET

BOLD JUMPING SPIDER

As I'm finishing lunch, Ava comes over.

A **black-capped chickadee** sings, and we look up.

I'm really curious about Ava's list. "Did you see the hummingbird moth?" I ask.

"No," she says. "Did you see the barred owl?"

"Not yet. What does it look like?" I ask.

Ava shows me the picture in her guidebook.

"I *really* want to see that!" I say. "Let's compare lists." Our team's is a little longer.

"I'm not worried," she says. "We'll catch up."

"Hey, look!" Ava shouts.

A **wood frog** hops across my foot. "That's good luck for Green," I say.

"We'll see," says Ava. "Now it's on both our lists."

"So is that!" I say, pointing to a **daddy longlegs** on Ava's arm. She shakes it off and runs back to join her team.

DADDY LONGLEGS

After lunch, we head deeper into the woods where it's boggy and wet. I see several downed logs in the clearing. "Can we roll one?" I ask.

"Sure!" says Ranger Kai. "But be careful. We need to respect the animals that live there."

We gently roll over a log. **Sowbugs**, **ground spiders**, and **carpenter ants** scurry for cover. A few **earthworms** and a **centipede** linger.

"Did you know centipedes never have exactly 100 legs?" I ask.

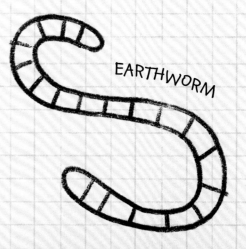

PILLBUG

EARTHWORM

After we replace the log as we found it, I see a bigger one with bright orange fungi. I just know it has something amazing underneath. "Can we roll this one, too?" I beg.

"Normally, we'd only move one log in an area to protect the wildlife," says Ranger Kai. "But this *is* a Bioblitz . . ."

Ranger Kai and I roll the second log, and I see what looks like a giant globby slug with spots. But wait, it's got feet—and a tail. "What's that?"

"Great find!" says Ranger Kai. "It's a **blue-spotted salamander**. We've never seen one in the park. Gabriel, put a star next to that one."

60 blue-spotted salamander ★

60

BLUE-SPOTTED SALAMANDER

"Let's walk down this forest path," says Ranger Kai.

A **garter snake** whips across the trail and vanishes under a bush. **Chipmunks** chase each other through pools of light. A **titmouse** flits from branch to branch.

"Jay! Jay! Jay!" a **blue jay** calls.

Suddenly, there's a loud rushing sound and we all freeze! A huge bird with wings as long as my arms glides above our heads.

"Someone's telling us it's time to leave," says Ranger Kai with a laugh.

I gaze at the dish-shaped face and unblinking eyes, just like the ones in the picture in Ava's guidebook. "Is it a **barred owl**?" I ask.

"You got it," says Ranger Kai.

I can't wait to tell Ava!

61

62

61 common garter snake

62 blue jay

63 tufted titmouse

64 eastern chipmunk

65 barred owl

BLUE JAY

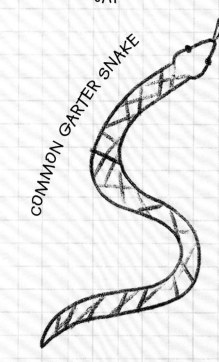

COMMON GARTER SNAKE

As we march out of the forest, the sun is sinking low. I scoop up a caterpillar. "Did you know **woolly bears** make their own antifreeze?"

Shadows on the lawn become a family of rabbits. "**Eastern cottontails**," says Mrs. Tatke.

"And someone to eat them," says Ranger Kai, when a **red fox** bounds across the grass. The rabbits dash away.

"Ow! **Mosquitoes**!" I swat at my arm. "And someone to eat *them*!" I say, watching the **little brown bats** flying overhead.

White-tailed deer appear at the edge of the woods. Ranger Kai asks everyone to gather close.

"Our Bioblitzing is almost done," she announces. "It's time to meet up with the Blue Team at the gazebo."

66 woolly bear caterpillar (Isabella tiger moth larva)

67 little brown bat

68 eastern cottontail

69 woodchuck

70 broad-winged hawk

71 green-striped grasshopper

72 mosquito

73 white-tailed deer

74 red fox

WOOLLY BEAR CATERPILLAR

A light shines in the gazebo. Dad's team is already there, standing next to a big white cloth hanging from a wire.

"What's up with the sheet?" I ask Ranger Kai.

"The bright light attracts the night insects," she says. "The white sheet allows us to see them!"

The sheet is covered with spots.

I run over for a closer look. "This is awesome. Look at the moths! Hey, Ava. Did you know some moths don't have mouths?"

"So they don't talk so much?" she teases.

"Ha ha! You'd better be glad I talk so much." I point to a reddish insect. "If I didn't, you wouldn't know that's a **ruby tiger moth**!"

75 crane fly
76 crambid snout moth
77 mayfly
78 leafhopper
79 Japanese beetle
80 ruby tiger moth
81 phantom midge
82 American idia moth
83 tawny cockroach

RUBY TIGER MOTH

Ava and I compare lists. "Our team found 83 species," I announce.

"Ours found 84," says Ava.

"Almost a tie." I guess it's okay if she wins. She *is* my cousin.

"I see you spotted my barred owl," Ava says.

"Yeah," I say. "I thought of you."

Ava looks at my list again. "What's a blue-spotted salamander?"

Just as I'm about to tell her, a black-and-white shape shuffles into the light. Did somebody's cat escape?

"Uh-oh," cries Dad. "**Skunk**! Nobody move."

"It must have been attracted to our insect buffet," I whisper as it ambles away.

"One more for the list! But your team still wins by one point, doesn't it, Dad?"

㊙ striped skunk

BARRED OWL

"Well, each team saw some animals the other one didn't," says Dad. "Together we saw a grand total of 100 species!"

"Wow, we needed everyone to make this Bioblitz a success," I say.

"We did," agrees Ranger Kai. "And I think you deserve a special award, Gabriel."

"Why?" I ask.

"You found the blue-spotted salamander," she says. "They're rare around here. We call them species of 'special concern.' Now that we know they're here, the park will get extra help to protect its animals!"

"That's great!" I shout. "Spring Meadow Park is the real winner!"

"Hooray for the Bioblitz!"

GABRIEL'S BIOBLITZ LIST

VERTEBRATES
(animals with *backbones*)

FISH
brown bullhead 27

AMPHIBIANS
American toad 5
blue-spotted salamander 60
green frog 32
wood frog 49

REPTILES
common garter snake 61
painted turtle 30

BIRDS
American goldfinch 25
American robin 2
barred owl 65
black-capped chickadee 47
blue jay 62
broad-winged hawk 70
brown creeper 46
chipping sparrow 1
house sparrow 4
mallard 28
pine warbler 45
red-bellied woodpecker 38
red-breasted nuthatch 42
rock pigeon 6
tufted titmouse 63

MAMMALS
eastern chipmunk 64
eastern cottontail 68
eastern gray squirrel 13
little brown bat 67
red fox 74
red squirrel 39
striped skunk 84
white-tailed deer 73
woodchuck 69

INVERTEBRATES
(animals without *backbones*)

ARACHNIDS (spiders, mites)
bold jumping spider 41
daddy longlegs 48
ground spider 54

INSECTS

Butterflies and moths
American idia moth 82
American lady 26
black swallowtail 14
cabbage white 16
clouded sulphur 24
crambid snout moth 76
eastern tiger swallowtail 19
great spangled fritillary 3
hummingbird moth 23
monarch 18
ruby tiger moth 80
woolly bear caterpillar
(Isabella tiger moth larva) 66

Other insects
aphid 15
Asian lady beetle 9
bald-faced hornet 22
brown marmorated stink bug 10
caddisfly (larva) 33
carpenter ant 59
common eastern bumblebee 21
common green darner 29
common water strider 34
conifer bark beetle 44
crane fly 75
deer fly 40
earwig 57
eastern carpenter bee 17
eastern pondhawk 35
eastern yellow jacket 43
field cricket 11
green-striped grasshopper 71

NOTE: *To see photos of these creatures in their natural habitats, visit inaturalist.org/observations.*

ACKNOWLEDGMENTS

The author wishes to thank Peter Alden for his commitment to biodiversity and his willingness to share his knowledge, Linda Graetz for shining a light on a "moth blitz" and Linda Hoffman for hosting it, and Tia Pinney for providing expert review of the book's animal and habitat science. I am deeply grateful to my wonderful agent, Stephen Fraser at the Jennifer de Chiara Literary Agency, for his belief in my work, and to Margaret Quinlin, Kathy Landwehr, and Vicky Holifield at Peachtree for welcoming these characters into their house. I am also indebted to the Concord, Massachusetts, chapter of the Society of Children's Book Writers and Illustrators, my beloved book family, for their unwavering support and generosity. Loving thanks to my parents, James and Nancy Edwards, and my brother, Jeff Edwards, for my childhood roots in nature, to my husband, Jim, for being my first and best reader, and to my dear daughters, Elana and Sonia, who are in my heart with every word I write.

GABRIEL'S "DID YOU KNOW . . . ?" FACTS

"Did you know some bugs are related to lobsters?"

Pillbugs, also known as roly-polys, are not insects, but instead members of the order Isopoda and the woodlouse family. Woodlice are land crustaceans, distant cousins of lobsters and shrimp. Sowbugs look a lot like pillbugs, but they have tail-like projections and can't roll into a ball!

"Did you know spittlebugs cover their eggs in bubbly spit?"

When meadow spittlebugs lay eggs on plants in August and September, they cover them with a frothy foam. The foam is easily seen but hides and protects the eggs beneath.

"Did you know some bugs look like birds?"

A hummingbird moth can be easily mistaken for a hummingbird at first glance. They are both pollinators who are drawn to flowers with deep cups, both dart quickly through the air, and both hover. But where hummingbirds are sleek and shiny with smooth heads, hummingbird moths are fuzzy looking with feathery antennae.

"Did you know an insect called the lacewing uses aphids' dead bodies for camouflage?"

Lacewings are insects that prey on aphids. The larva puncture the aphids with hollow mandibles and suck out their meal, leaving husks of their insect prey. Some lacewing species have sharp hairs on their backs and stick these insect husks on the hairs to hide themselves when hunting the unsuspecting aphids.

"Did you know a jumping spider has four pairs of eyes?"

Jumping spiders have one large pair of eyes in the middle of their faces, and a smaller eye on either side in front. There's another set toward the middle, and a rear-facing pair looking backward. Because spiders can't turn their heads, they need eyes to see and sense motion all around them.

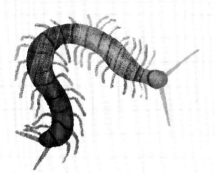

"Did you know centipedes never have exactly 100 legs?"

Centipedes always have an odd number of leg pairs. The number of pairs can range from 15 to 191 but only odd numbers. Scientists are still studying why. Fun fact: Centipedes can also regenerate legs.

"Did you know some moths don't have mouths?"

Some species of moths, such as the luna moth, do not have mouths, so these insects cannot eat in their adult stage. They eat enough while they are caterpillars, and live as adult moths only long enough to lay their eggs.

"Did you know that woolly bears make their own antifreeze?"

Two, or sometimes three, generations of woolly bears hatch, molt, and pupate in a single year, but the last generation has the remarkable ability to overwinter. It hibernates by producing an antifreeze called glycerol, which allows everything but the interior of its cells to freeze.

Author's Note

I participated as a community scientist in bird counts for about ten years before I first learned about biodiversity counts, or **Bioblitzes**. How exciting to take an inventory of *all* the kinds of living things, or *species*, in an area, not just a single group like birds. When I discovered that Concord, Massachusetts, a town near my home, had hosted a number of biodiversity counts, I knew I had to learn more!

A Bioblitz can include animals, plants, and fungi—or it can target a single group of organisms, such as butterflies or moths. *Bioblitz!* focuses on animals, because they're easier for most people to identify. Also, because animals move around, they are especially exciting to spot. The groups of animals included in this book are divided into *vertebrates*, animals that have a backbone, and *invertebrates*, animals that don't. Although most people are more familiar with vertebrate species—perhaps because we are one!—approximately 95 percent of animal species are invertebrate.

The first recorded Bioblitz was held in Kenilworth Park & Aquatic Gardens in Washington, DC, on May 31, 1996.

Scientists, together with community volunteers, found and identified close to a thousand species in a 24-hour period. A Bioblitz often includes a range of experts to document all the species found. Scientists specializing in insects (*entomologists*), birds (*ornithologists*), and reptiles and amphibians (*herpetologists*) are a few of the experts who might be represented. Volunteers acting as community scientists, like Gabriel and Ava, are invaluable in gathering data.

Now held all over the world in ecosystems as diverse as wildlife refuges and city parks, Bioblitzes are important tools for learning about the health and biodiversity of an area. During a Bioblitz, people might discover an endangered or threatened species, or one of special concern, as Gabriel did, and share this information with local, state, or federal agencies. The collected data also might be used to learn about the effects of habitat loss, invasive species, and climate change. But most importantly, a Bioblitz is a wonderful way to bring a community together in order to better appreciate the natural environment in which we live.

If you are interested in participating in a Bioblitz in your area, look for field guides to your own region. The following resources are also helpful:

Alden, Peter, and Brian Cassie. *National Audubon Society Field Guide to New England*. New York: Knopf, 2018. An overview of the natural history of New England including photos and descriptions of many of the animals in the book.

See the National Audubon Society website for comprehensive field guides for eight geographic regions of North America. *www.audubon.org/audubon-regional-field-guides/*

National Audubon Society also offers numerous field guides focusing on specific animal and plant groups. *www.audubon.org/national-audubon-society-field-guides/*

BioBlitz and iNaturalist: Counting Species Through Citizen Science. National Geographic's BioBlitz Guide is a how-to resource for planning and carrying out your own event. *www.nationalgeographic.org/projects/bioblitz/*

The Great Walden BioBlitz. In 2019 the Walden Woods Project, Minute Man National Historical Park, the E.O. Wilson Biodiversity Foundation, and naturalist Peter Alden held their third event documenting the biodiversity within a 5-mile radius of Walden Pond in Concord, Massachusetts. *www.walden.org/explore-walden-woods/great-walden-bioblitz/*

iNaturalist. A joint initiative of the California Academy of Sciences and National Geographic, iNaturalist is a web application that allows you to record your wildlife findings, identify what you find, and share your discoveries with others. *www.inaturalist.org/*

Schoolyard Bioblitz Education Kit, Nature NB. A step-by-step resource guide about how to incorporate bioblitzes into a teaching curriculum. *www.naturenb.ca/wp-content/uploads/2018/07/Bioblitz-Kit-Elementary-School-EN.pdf*